Happy
Easter '98
Lots of Love
Auntie C.
xxx

This book belongs to

Lauren x

2003
LQ※

The Little Mermaid

BY

Hans Christian Andersen

Retold by Jennifer Greenway

ILLUSTRATED BY

Robyn Officer

LEOPARD

This edition published in 1995 by Leopard Books,
20 Vauxhall Bridge Road, London SW1V 2SA

First published in 1992 by Andrews and McMeel

ISBN 0 7529 0118 4

Design: Susan Hood and Mike Hortens
Art Direction: Armand Eisen, Mike Hortens and Julie Phillips
Art Production: Lynn Wine
Production: Julie Miller and Lisa Shadid

The
Little Mermaid

$\mathcal{D}$eep in the blue sparkling ocean, deeper than any human has ever gone, the Sea King lived with his subjects in a splendid palace made of rare seashells and pearls.

Now, the Sea King had six beautiful mermaid daughters. The youngest one was the most beautiful. And she was much quieter and more thoughtful than her sisters.

While her sisters enjoyed
playing with silvery fish
and making wreaths
of coloured seaweed,
the youngest found no
amusement in such games.
She liked more than
anything to hear
of the world above
the sea, and she often
asked her grandmother
what it was like.

The little mermaid loved to hear how
flowers on land had a fragrance—so
different from those under the water,
which had none. She was also delighted to
learn that the fishes on land—for that's what
grandmother called birds—sang beautiful
songs. But best of all she liked to hear about
the human beings who lived in the world
above the waves.

When the daughters of the Sea King reached their fifteenth year, they were allowed to go to the surface of the water. But the little mermaid, being the youngest, watched all her sisters go before her.

When the oldest sister came back, she spoke of the twinkling stars. The second described a beautiful sunset. The third saw a garden full of flowers. The fourth told about the vast blue sky, and the fifth was amazed by giant pale icebergs floating in the ocean. Yet despite the wonderful sights above the water, all the little mermaid's sisters agreed that the world beneath the waves was far more beautiful.

"I shall have to see for myself," the little mermaid thought wistfully. "How I wish my turn would come."

At last, the little mermaid's fifteenth birthday came, and up she went to the world above the waves.

It was evening and the sky sparkled with silver stars. A ship lit with coloured lanterns sailed toward the little mermaid. The people on board were having a party. The little mermaid swam up and peered through the window of one of the cabins.

Inside she saw a handsome prince laughing and talking with his friends. He had just turned sixteen years old, and the party was in honour of his birthday.

The little mermaid fell in love with him at once. "If only he could see me," she thought, "perhaps he would love me, too."

Just then the little mermaid saw that a terrible storm was blowing up. The waves began rising higher and higher, and the wind whistled. Soon the ship began to creak and groan. "We're going to sink!" the little mermaid heard one of the sailors yell.

Finally the ship began breaking apart, and everyone on board was cast into the water. At first, the little mermaid was glad, since now the handsome prince would be with her. Then she remembered that humans could not live underwater.

"I must save him!" the little mermaid thought. She dove again and again. At last, she found the prince deep beneath the waves. He was still alive.

She pulled him to the surface. She held his head above the water, and they drifted all night.

By dawn, the storm had passed and the
little mermaid saw a quiet beach. Just
beyond the beach, a white church nestled
on a hill. She swam to the shore while still
holding the prince and dragged him onto
the sand. She kissed him on the forehead,
but he did not wake up.

Then the church bell rang and a group of
young women ran out of the church door.
The sound of their voices frightened the
little mermaid and she hid behind a rock.

One of the young women ran onto the
beach and up to the prince as he was
opening his eyes. She was very beautiful,
and the prince smiled at her.

"You have saved my life!" he said, for he did not know it was the little mermaid who had really saved him.

Then the young woman helped the prince to his feet and led him away to the white church.

The little mermaid sighed and swam under the waves back to her father's palace. When her sisters asked her what she had seen above the waves, she would not answer. But day and night she thought of the handsome prince, and she grew sad and pale.

The little mermaid began to spend all her time roaming the world above the waves looking for the prince.

One day, she came to a beach where a large marble palace stood. To her joy, she saw the prince walking along the shore, for this palace was his.

After that the little mermaid came every day to secretly watch the prince. Her love for him grew. But she dared not show herself, because her grandmother had told her that humans were afraid of mermaids.

"They believe that everyone should have two of those props they call legs," her grandmother had said. "And they think our tails are very ugly!"

"Ah, if only I had legs," the little mermaid thought. "Perhaps then I could make the prince love me!" Then the little mermaid decided to do a terrible thing.

In the very depths of the ocean, there lived an ancient sea witch. She was wicked but very powerful. So the little mermaid went to seek her advice.

When the little mermaid entered the sea witch's cave, the sea witch stared at her and cackled. "I know why you have come, foolish princess," she said. "I can give you legs, but it will not be easy for you. You will be as graceful as you are now, but each step you take will feel as if you are treading on sharp knives!"

"I do not mind," replied the little mermaid, thinking only of the prince.

"There is more," the sea witch went on. "Once you have taken a human form, you will never be able to live with your family under the waves again. Moreover, if the prince does not love you in return and agree to marry you, you will perish. The morning after he marries another, your heart will break and you will be nothing—only the foam on the waves!"

The little mermaid turned pale. "I will still do it," she said.

"But I must be paid," said the sea witch. "In return for giving you legs I must have your voice."

The little mermaid faltered. Her voice was the loveliest of all the sea creatures, and far more beautiful than that of any mortal. "But how will I make the prince love me without my voice!" she cried.

"You are very lovely," said the witch. "Use that to charm him."

"Very well," said the little mermaid.

So the little mermaid gave her voice to the sea witch, and in return the sea witch gave her the magic potion that would make her legs.

The little mermaid waited until
night and sadly bid farewell to her
sleeping father, grandmother, and
sisters. Then she swam to the beach
near the prince's palace and swallowed
the sea witch's potion.

She felt as if a sword had been passed
through her, and she fainted. When she
awoke it was morning, and to her surprise
the prince was standing over her. The little
mermaid looked down and saw that she had
two pretty legs and dainty feet.

"Who are you?" the prince asked, but the
little mermaid could not answer.
She was so lovely and her blue
eyes looked so sad that the
prince took pity on her and
led her to his palace.

As the sea witch had promised, every step the little mermaid took was as painful as stepping on sharp knives. But she bore it bravely.

The prince ordered his servants to dress her in fine robes. When this was done, the little mermaid was the most beautiful young woman in the palace. Yet she still could not utter a word, only stare at the prince with her sad, blue eyes.

"You poor creature," the prince said. "If only you could speak to me. You remind me of a girl I met once who saved my life when I almost drowned. She is the only woman I can ever love, but I shall never see her again.

22

So will you stay with me instead?"

When she heard that, the little mermaid's heart almost broke. She wished she could tell the prince that it was she who had saved his life. But she could not say a word.

The prince made the little mermaid his closest companion. She did all she could to please him, but he spoke only of the one who had saved him. "I shall never see her again," he told the little mermaid. "But I am glad that you at least have been sent to me, my beautiful silent friend."

Then the little mermaid danced for him, though it hurt her terribly. She danced so gracefully the prince was enchanted and said she must stay with him always.

One day the king announced that the prince must marry the daughter of the neighbouring king. The prince told the little mermaid that he would never do so. "I cannot marry that princess when I love only the girl who saved me," he said. "I would rather marry you than anyone but her." Then he kissed the little mermaid on the cheek.

The next day the king prepared a ship to travel to the nearby kingdom. The little mermaid accompanied the prince on the journey.

When the ship reached the shore, the neighbouring king and the princess were there to greet them.

When the prince saw the princess, he cried, "But she is the one who saved my life! All my wishes have come true!" As soon as he was on land, he ran to the princess, leaving the little mermaid standing alone.

The princess was very beautiful and her eyes were kind and gentle. The little mermaid stared at her. "She is lovely and she seems good," the mermaid thought. "The prince loves her, for how can he know that it was I who saved his life and not she? So now I must prepare to die."

The wedding of the prince and the princess was celebrated that very night.

The prince asked the little mermaid to stand close to him during the wedding. "You must share in my happiness," he said. So the little mermaid held up the bride's veil and smiled, even though her heart was broken.

"Tomorrow I must die," she thought. "I will never see my dear sisters or my father or grandmother again!" And a tear rolled down her cheek.

Late that night the prince and his bride went to bed on the ship that was to carry them back to the prince's kingdom. Meanwhile, the little mermaid stood on the deck and gazed at the sea.

Then she saw her sisters swimming toward her. Their beautiful long hair had all been cut off. The eldest one carried a sharp knife in her hand. They were all weeping as they called to the little mermaid, "Dear sister, we gave our hair to the sea witch in exchange for this knife. Before the sun rises, you must kill the prince with it. Then your legs will disappear and your tail will grow back. After that you may come and live with us under the waves again!"

28

The little mermaid took the knife and went inside the ship to the prince's room. He lay there asleep beside his bride.

When she saw him, tears came to the little mermaid's eyes, and she ran to the deck and flung the knife into the sea. Then as the sun was rising, she threw herself into the water. She waited to die and become like the foam on the waves. But instead she felt herself being lifted high into the air.

"Where am I?" she cried.

"You are with us, the spirits of the air," replied a host of musical voices. "Because of your good deed, little mermaid, you have been made one of us. You will not die. Instead you will travel around the world spreading peace and kindness, and you will live with us forever."

The little mermaid felt full of joy. Looking down, she saw the prince gazing sadly into the water as if he were looking for her. She flew down to him and whispered, "Do not be sad! All is well!"

As the prince's face grew peaceful again, the little mermaid joined hands with the other spirits of the air and rose into the clouds.

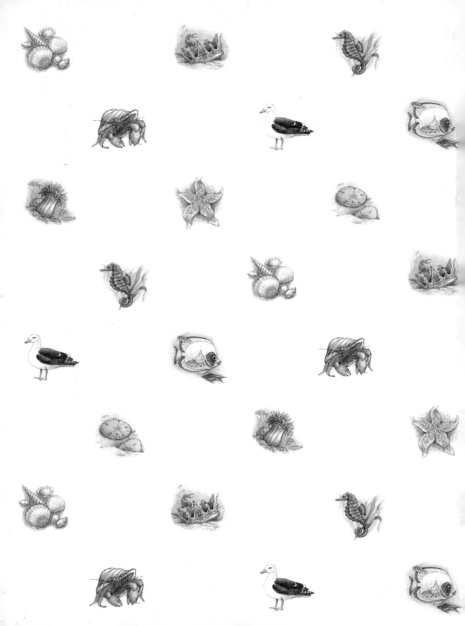